JAPANESE FAIRY TALES

First Series

&

Second Series

Retold by

Teresa Peirce Williston

The Rōnin's Collection of Old Books

JAPANESE
FAIRY TALES

First Series

Retold by

Teresa Peirce Williston

1904

THE PREFACE

To retell any of the stories of the Orient to the children of the Occident and preserve all the original flavor and charm, would be impossible. Still there is much in the story, just as a story, to delight little readers of America, as well as to broaden their sympathies and stimulate new ideas. And our practical little Jonathans and Columbias need a touch of the imagination and poetry embodied in these tales, which have been treasured through hundreds of years by the little ones of Japan.

Every effort has been made to bring Japanese life as vividly as possible before the children by means of the illustrations. Mr. Ogawa, the illustrator, is a native of Japan and a graduate of the Imperial Art School of Tokyo, and combines the Japanese artistic instinct and classic tradition with a knowledge of American ideas and methods.

To Mr. Katayama of Tokyo I am indebted for great assistance in collecting these stories.

T. P. W.

September, 1904

THE WONDERFUL TEAKETTLE

The old priest was very happy. He had found a new treasure. As he climbed the hill to the temple where he lived, he often stopped to pat his beautiful brass teakettle. When he reached the temple he called the three boys who were his pupils.

"See here!" he cried to them. "Just see the beautiful kettle I found in a little shop I passed. I got it very cheap, too." The boys admired it, but smiled a little to themselves, for they could not see what he wanted of an old brass kettle.

"Now you go on with your studies," said the priest. "I will hear you recite after a while." So the boys went into the next room, and the old priest sat down to admire his prize. He sat and looked at it so long that he grew sleepy, and nod, bob, went his head until in a moment he was fast asleep.

The boys in the next room studied very hard for a few minutes, but they were boys, and no one was there to see to them, so you can imagine what they were doing by the time the priest was well asleep.

Suddenly" they heard a noise in the next room.

"There, the priest is awake," whispered one.

"Oh, dear! Now we'll have to behave," said the second.

The third one was more daring. He crept up and peeped through the screen, to see if it really was the priest. He was just in time to see the new teakettle give a spring into the air, turn a somersault, and come down a furry little badger with a sharp nose, bushy tail, and four little feet.

How that badger did caper and dance! It danced on the floor. It danced on the table. It danced up the side of a screen. "Oh, my! Oh, my!" cried the boy, tumbling back. "It will dance on me next! Oh, my! "

"What are you talking about?" said the other two. "What will dance on you?"

"That goblin will dance on me. I know it will! It danced on the floor and it danced on the table and it danced on the screen, and now I know it is coming to dance on me!" said the boy.

"What do you mean?" said the others. "There is no goblin here." Then they, too, looked through the screen. There sat the kettle just as it had been before.

"You little silly!" cried one of the other boys. "Do you call that a goblin? That looks very much like a teakettle to my eyes."

"Hush!" said the third boy. "The priest is waking up. We had better get to work again."

The priest waked up and heard the busy lips of his pupils. "What good boys I have!" he thought. "Now while they are working I will just brew myself a cup of tea."

He lighted his little charcoal fire, filled his kettle with fresh water, and put it over the fire to heat.

Suddenly the kettle gave a leap up into the air, spilling the hot water all over the floor. "Hot, hot! I am burning," it cried, and like a flash it was no longer a kettle, but a little furry badger with a sharp nose, bushy tail, and four little feet.

"Oh, help! Oh, help! Here is a goblin!" shrieked the priest. In rushed the three boys to see what was the matter. They saw no kettle at all, but in its place was a very angry badger prancing and sputtering about the room.

They all took sticks and began to beat the badger, but it was again only a brass kettle that answered "Clang, clang!" to every blow.

When the priest saw that he could gain nothing by beating the kettle he began to plan how he might get rid of it. Just then the tinker came by.

"That is my chance," thought the priest, so he called, "Tinker, tinker, come and see what I have for you. Here is an old kettle I found. It is no use to me, but you could mend it up and sell it."

The tinker saw that it was a good kettle, so he bought it and took it home. He pressed it carefully into shape again, and mended all the broken places. Once more it was a fine-looking kettle.

That night the tinker awoke and found a badger looking at him with his small bright eyes.

"Now see here, Mr. Tinker," said the badger; "I think that you are a kind man, so I have something to tell you. I am really a wonderful teakettle, and can turn into a badger whenever I wish, as you see. I can do other things, too, more wonderful than that."

The kind-hearted tinker said: "Well, if you are a badger you must want something to eat. What can I get for you?" "Oh, I like a little sugar now and then," replied the badger, "and I don't like to be set on the fire or beaten with sticks. But I am sure that you will never treat me that way. If you wish to take me around, to the different villages, I can sing and dance on the tight rope for you."

The tinker did this, and crowds came to see the wonderful kettle. Those who had seen it once came again, and. those who had not seen it came to see why the people liked it so well.

At last the tinker became rich. Then he put his beloved teakettle in a little temple on the top of a hill, where it might always rest and have all the sugar-plums it wanted.

THE WOOD-CUTTER'S SAKE

The sun was just rising behind the hills. The great pine trees showed each black needle against the rosy clouds of sunrise. The stones along the pathway looked orange in the sunshine and purple in the shadow. The dew-wet breeze blew sweet and fresh over the rice fields.

A poor wood-cutter was toiling up the mountain side. Every morning, almost before the sun was up, he might be seen climbing to the wooded top of the mountain. No one worked so hard as this poor wood-cutter, yet no matter how hard he worked, there was never enough wood in his pile at night to please him.

This morning, as he walked along, he talked to himself. "It seems to make no difference how early I start or how late I work at night, I never have enough money to buy the things I wish for my old father and mother. Now at their age they need tea and sometimes a cup of sake."

So he set to work harder than before. It was very warm and he was very tired as well as hungry. Suddenly close by where he was chopping he saw a fat young badger fast asleep.

"Well!" thought the wood-cutter, "here is something I might take home to my father and mother. He would make a hue stew."

The more he looked at the sleeping badger the less he wanted to kill him. If he were awake it would be different, but to kill him asleep! The wood-cutter could not do it.

He said to himself, "No, I cannot kill him. I will just work harder, and see if I cannot earn money enough to buy them something extra for to-morrow."

Just then the badger stood up. He did not run away as you might expect. He stood looking at the man. It almost seemed as though he smiled.

The wood-cutter stared at him with his mouth open. You do not expect the badger you are just going to kill to stand and smile at you. But this badger spoke, and this is what he said: "Now, Mr. Wood-cutter, you did well not to kill me. In the first place you could not do it. More than that, since you were good to me, I will be good to you. You cannot guess all the things I can do for you.

But first, will you just go beyond that pine tree and bring me a smooth flat stone you find there."

The wood-cutter hurried to get the stone. When he reached the place there lay a rich feast all spread out on dainty dishes.

The wood-cutter thought of his father and mother. He wished he might take them just a bite of some of these dainties. He would not touch anything that was not his own, however, so he began to look for a smooth flat stone.

"He-he!" chuckled some one behind him. He looked around. It was the badger, laughing until his bushy tail shook.

"Does it not look good? Why don't you eat some?"

"Oh, I did not wish any for myself. I only wished that my poor old father and mother might have such a feast as that for once in their lives."

"Never mind, they are eating just such a one this minute."

The wood-cutter stared. "Why, we have only rice and water in the house," he said.

"They are eating just what you see here," said the badger.

"Where could they get it?"

"I sent it to them, and this is for you and me. So sit down quickly, for I am very hungry."

They sat down and ate and ate, now *dango*, or dumpling, now *gozen*, or boiled rice. Then eggplant, sake, cakes, and fruits until the wood-cutter could eat no more.

The badger looked like a round fat dumpling himself, he was so full. "Rap-a-tap, rap-a-tap, rap-a-tap, rap. Rub-a-dub, rub-a-dub, rub-a-dub, rap."

It sounded like the music of the drum beating for the soldiers.

"Fan-ta-ra-ra-ra, fan-ta-ra-ra."

This was like the music for the dances.

"Ru-lo, re-lo, ru-le-o, re-lo."

It was the wailing of the sad sweet *samisen*. Where did it all come from? The woodcutter was looking everywhere but the right place. "Where does all this sweet music come from?" he asked the badger. Then he saw.

It was the badger drumming and strumming on his skin that was stretched until he looked like a dumpling.

With a chuckle the badger disappeared. The woodcutter looked for him, but saw only a beautiful waterfall. It tumbled in foam over the rocks. What a sweet song it sang!

The wood-cutter knew that he had never seen it before. He went up to look at it. Sniff! Something smelled very good. He stooped down to drink of the cold sparkling water.

He drank and stared, then drank again. It was sake, as sure as could be. He filled his gourd with it and hastened home.

"Father, here is some sake for you!" he cried.

He told his father all about the badger and the feast. Then his father told him about his feast, too.

The next morning when he started to work, you may be sure he did not forget his gourd. He was surprised to see a great crowd of people going tip the mountain. Before this he was the only one who would take that long, hard climb. They all had gourds in their hands, as many as they could carry.

Some one had listened at the wood-cutter's door the evening before, and heard him tell about the sake waterfall.

When they reached the place one of the men said: "Now, young man, since we happen to know about this place, you need not mind if we help ourselves first. We have to go back down the mountain to our work, so we are in a hurry. First, let us all have a drink together."

They all filled their gourds and took a long, deep drink. How they stared! The wood-cutter saw that something was wrong, so he slipped away and hid behind a big pine tree.

They took one more taste, "Water! That is only water!" all shouted at once. "Just wait until we get that scamp!" But they could not find him anywhere.

Down the hill they went again. They were angry to think of that long walk for nothing.

When they were gone the wood-cutter slipped out and tasted the water again. It was sake, just as before.

After that, whenever the poor wood-cutter went there for a drink, or to fill the gourd for his father, the water tasted like the richest   sake,   but   for   others   it   was   only   water.

THE MIRROR OF MATSUYAMA

In Matsuyama there lived a man, his wife, and their little daughter. They loved each other very much, and were very happy together. One day the man came home very sad. He had received a message from the Emperor, which said that he must take a journey to far-off Tokyo.

They had no horses and in those days there were no railroads in Japan. The man knew that he must walk the whole distance. It was not the long walk that he minded, however. It was because it would take him many days from home.

Still he must obey his Emperor, so he made ready to start. His wife was very sorry that he must go, and yet a little proud, too, for no one else in the village had ever taken so long a journey.

She and the baby walked with him down to the turn in the road. There they stood and watched him through their tears, as he followed the path up through the pines on the mountain side. At last, no larger than a speck, he disappeared behind the hills. Then they went home to await his return.

For three long weeks they waited. Each day they spoke of him, and counted the days until they should his dear face again. At last time came. They walked down to the turn in the road to wait for his coming. Up on the mountain side some one was walking toward them. As he came nearer they could see that it was the one for whom they waited.

The good wife could scarcely believe that her husband was indeed safe home again. The baby girl laughed and clapped her hands to see the toys he brought her.

There was a tiny image of Uzume, the laughter-loving goddess. Next came a little red monkey of cotton, with a blue head. When she pressed the spring he ran to the top of the rod. Oh, how wonderful was the third gift! It was a *tombo*, or dragon fly. When she first looked at it she saw only a piece of wood shaped like T. The cross piece was painted with different bright colors. But the queer thing, when her father twirled it between his fingers, would rise in the air, dipping and hovering like a real dragon fly.

Last, of course, there was a *ninghio*, or doll, with a sweet face, slanting eyes, and such wonderful hair. Her name was O-Hina-San. He told of the Feast of the Dead which he had seen in Tokyo.

He told of the beautiful lanterns, the Lanterns of the Dead; and the pine torches burning before each house. He told of the tiny boats made of barley straw and filled with food that are set floating away on the river, bearing two tiny lanterns to guide them to the Land of the Dead.

At last her husband handed the wife a small white box. "Tell me what you see inside," he said. She opened it and took out something round and bright.

On one side were buds and flowers of frosted silver. The other side at first looked as clear and bright as a pool of water. When she moved it a little she saw in it a most beautiful woman.

"Oh, what a beautiful picture!" she cried. "It is of a woman and she seems to be smiling and talking just as I am. She has on a blue dress just like mine, too! How strange!"

Then her husband laughed and said:

"That is a mirror. It is yourself you see reflected in it. All the women in Tokyo have them."

The wife was delighted with her present, and looked at it very often. She liked to see the smiling red lips, the laughing eyes, and beautiful dark hair.

After a while she said to herself: "How foolish this is of me to sit and gaze at myself in this mirror! I am not more beautiful than other women. How much better for me to enjoy others' beauty and forget my own face. I shall only remember that it must always be happy and smiling or it will make no one else happy. I do not wish any cross or angry look of mine to make anyone sad."

She put the mirror carefully away in its box. Only twice in a year she looked at it. Then it was to see if her face was still such as would make others happy.

The years passed by in their sweet and simple life until the baby had grown to be a big girl. Her *ninghio*, her *tombo*, the image of Uzume, even the cotton monkey, were put carefully away for her own children.

This girl was the very image of her mother. She was just as sweet and loving, just as kind and helpful.

One day her mother became very ill. Although the girl and her father did all they could for her, she grew worse and worse.

At last she knew that she must die, so she called her daughter to her and said: "My child, I know that I must soon leave you, but I wish to leave something with you in my place. Open this box and see what you find in it."

The girl opened the box and looked for the first time in a mirror. "Oh, mother dear!" she cried. "I see you here. Not thin and pale as you are now, but happy and smiling, as you have always been."

Then her mother said: "When I am gone, will you look in this every morning and every night? If anything troubles you, tell me about it. Always try to do right, so that you will see only happiness here."

Every morning when the sun rose and the birds began to twitter and sing, the girl rose and looked in her mirror. There she saw the bright, happy face that she remembered as her mother's.

Every evening when the shadows fell and the birds were asleep, she looked again. She told it all that had happened during the day. When it had been a happy day the face smiled back at her. When she was sad the face looked sad, too. She was very .careful not to do anything unkind, for she knew how sad the face would be then.

So each day she grew more kind and loving, and more like the mother whose face she saw each day and loved.

THE EIGHT-HEADED SERPENT

The great god Susano walked by the river Hi. He walked for four days and saw no living thing. At evening on the fifth day he lay down to sleep in the bamboo thicket, close by the river's edge.

He dreamed that he saw a beautiful maiden floating down the river. A great monster rose from the water and was about to swallow her, but the god swam out and saved her.

Susano wondered about his dream, and in the morning he said to himself "In this beautiful land it seems strange that I find no living thing. I will go on up the river today but if by night I find no one, I will return to heaven once more."

As he spoke something floated down the blue face of the river. It was a chop-stick. Then the god Susano knew that some one lived by the river, so he started on to search until he found them.

Toward evening he thought he heard the sound of voices. He hurried on, and as he turned a bend in the river he saw an old woman sitting by the edge of the water and weeping. Her husband and little daughter sat near her.

Susano looked at the girl in surprise, for she seemed to be the same one whom he had seen in his dream.

"What is your trouble?" he asked of the woman. "Perhaps I can help you."

The old woman answered: "No one can help us. Our beautiful daughter must go as her seven beautiful sisters have gone."

"But tell me all about it," said Susano, for he remembered how he had saved the maiden in his dream.

"There is a great monster who owns all this land," said the man. "He is a serpent eight miles long, and he has eight heads and eight tails. Each year, for seven years, he has come and carried off one of our daughters. Now there is only this one, the youngest, remaining. We know that he will soon come and carry her away too. Nothing can save her."

Now Susano thought that so beautiful a maiden was too good for an eight-headed serpent, so he sat down and thought how he might save her. He sat by the river bank, under the feathery bamboo, and thought.

The blue face of the river turned to red and gold. Then Susano knew that the sun had set, but he did not look up. The light faded and all was dark. He knew the stars were shining, for he could see their tiny points of light reflected on the smooth surface of the water. Still he could think of no plan.

At last he said: "Morning thoughts are best. I will sleep now, and perhaps in the morning I can think of some plan."

In the morning he was up with the first light of the sun. The old woman brought him food, but he ate nothing. He sat by the water's edge, under the feathery bamboo, and thought and thought.

Just as the sun was sinking again he went to the old man and woman.

"Weep no more," he said. "I have thought of a plan to save your daughter. We will get up early in the morning and go to work, but to-night we will sleep, for we need rest."

The next morning they were at work long before light. The old woman prepared a rich soup in eight huge kettles. Susano and the old man made a great wall, having eight gates in it. Before each gate they set a kettle of the soup. Then Susano bruised some leaves which he found by the riverside and put them in the soup. A delicious odor arose from each kettle of soup and floated over the mountains.

Very soon they heard a great roar. "Be quick! Hide yourself!" cried the old man. "It is the eight-headed serpent. He has smelled the soup and is coming to get some."

With a noise like thunder the great serpent dragged himself over eight hills. His eight tails writhed along the ground or whipped through the air. Eight red tongues darted from his eight great mouths.

His eight heads poked through the eight gates in the wall, and in a moment the soup was disappearing.

Susano stole up, and with one blow of his sword cut off the first head of the serpent. In a moment another head was gone, then another and another.

The serpent was angry, but he would rather lose a few heads than forego the soup. Perhaps Susano had put something in the soup to make him think so.

Whiz! And the tails lashed about. Whiz! And Susano's sharp sword cut off the fifth head. The snake was furious with pain, but still trying to get the last few drops of soup that were left.

Susano's sharp sword flashed through the air and cut off the sixth head. Another moment and the seventh head fell.

Just then the serpent turned on Susano. His great mouth was open to swallow him, but the brave man sprang upon the monster's neck and from above cut off the last head.

The great body quivered and shook until the trembling leaves fell down from the trees. At last it lay quite still, and they knew that the serpent would never trouble them again.

Then Susano took the maiden up to the Land of the Smiling Heaven. There they lived, always looking down upon the earth to see who were in trouble and helping them.

THE STOLEN CHARM

A little boy sat on the sand at the foot of an old pine tree.

"Pish, pish," whispered the pine tree as the spring wind swept through its needles.

"Swish, swish," said the waves as they chased each other up to the yellow sand. "Swish, swish," said each wave as it threw its armful of white foam at the foot of the boy

The boy heard the whisper of the pine tree and the splash of the waves, but he looked far out over the water. He was looking for the white Foam Fairy who came each day to play with him.

At last she came, riding on the top of the highest wave. In her hand she held something which shone in the sun like a drop of dew.

She sat down on the sand with the boy. For a long time she sat watching the waves and the sea birds and the soft white clouds.

At last she said: "Little boy we have played here together for many weeks. Now I must go away to another land, so I have come to say good-by. Do you see this tiny silver ship I have brought you? It is a charm and will always keep you well and happy."

The boy looked up to say good-by, but could see only the rainbow that gleamed in the spray of the waves.

She was gone, but close by his hand lay a tiny silver ship that shone in the sun like a drop of dew. The boy picked it up and walked slowly to his home.

"See, mother," he said, "here is a tiny silver ship which the Foam Fairy gave to me."

"That is a charm, my boy," said his mother. "You must always keep it, for it is very precious."

Then he showed the charm to his two pets, the furry little Fox-cub and the fuzzy little Puppy. They sniffed and blinked at it very wisely as though they knew all about it.

Weeks passed and spring warmed into summer. One evening the boy became very ill. His mother went to fetch the silver charm, for that would make him well again. It was gone! Who could have taken it?

The furry little Fox-cub and the fuzzy little Puppy were very sad.

They sat in the dusk and blinked at the fireflies flashing among the trees. They blinked at the stars in the faraway sky. Their sharp little noses twitched as they smelled the sweet dew on the flowers.

They thought of their poor sick master and wondered how they could help him. At last the Fox-cub said: "I believe the Ogre must have stolen the charm. Let's go and see."

"Oh, dear! I'm afraid of ogres," said the Puppy with her tail between her legs. "How would we ever get it if he did have it?"

"Come along. We'll find a way," said the Fox-cub.

They crept softly along the path which led up the hill to the house of the Ogre. On the way they met the Rat.

"Where are you going?" squealed the Rat.

"We are going to the house of the Ogre, to see if he has stolen our master's charm," said the Fox-cub.

"And I don't know how we'll ever get it if he has it," whined the Puppy, with her tail between her legs.

"I'll go, too," said the Rat. "I know how you can get it. Just you wait here by this tree until I creep up to the house. When I am by the window you make a dreadful noise and then run for your lives. I'll meet you at the foot of the hill."

"Oh, dear! I'm afraid," sniffed the Puppy.

"Never mind, he won't hurt you," said the Fox-cub.

They waited by the pine tree until the Rat was close to the house. Then they made a noise like all sorts of monsters, and turned and ran for their lives.

By and by the Rat came, too.

"I know where it is!" he cried. "He has the charm and he keeps it in the pocket of his sleeve. I know it is there, for when you screamed he felt in his pocket the first thing to see that it was safe. Now we'll wait till he gets over being frightened, and then we'll go back and get it."

Soon they were by the pine tree again. Then the Rat said: "Now, you Fox-cub, change yourself into a little boy, and Puppy, into a little girl. Then both go in and dance for the Ogre. Dance for your lives, and keep dancing until I am down the hill again."

"Oh, dear! I'm so afraid of ogres," said the Puppy.

"Never mind. Dance for your life and he won't hurt you," said the Fox-cub.

Then the Rat hid himself in the folds of the girl's long dress. The boy and the girl walked up to the door of the house.

"Please, Mr. Ogre, may we dance for you?" they asked.

Now the Ogre was very tired and very cross, so a dance was just what he wanted to see. He said: "Yes, but if you don't dance well, I'll eat you."

They danced their very best and the Ogre was so interested that he did not see the little Rat slip from the girl's dress and crawl under his sleeve.

He did not hear the Rat gnaw through the cloth, nor see him as he slipped away with the tiny silver ship in his mouth.

When the Rat was safely down the hill, the girl and boy suddenly disappeared. The Ogre never knew what became of them. Like a flash they were only a Fox-cub and a Puppy, running and tumbling down the hill as fast as they could.

They thanked the Rat for his help, and then ran to their master with the silver ship. "Dear master!" they cried, "Here is your charm. Now you will be well once more."

Sure enough the boy did get well and lived long after the furry little Fox-cub was a grown-up Fox and the fuzz}' little Puppy was a grandmother Dog. But the Dog still puts her tail between her legs whenever you talk about ogres.

URASHIMA

Many years ago a boy lived down by the sea, where the great green waves came riding in to break on the shore in clouds of salty spray. This boy, Urashima, loved the water as a brother, and was often out in his boat from purple dawn to russet evening. One day as he was fishing, something tugged at his line, and he pulled in. It was not a fish, as he expected, but a wrinkled old turtle.

"Well," said Urashima, "if I cannot get a fish for my dinner, at least I will not keep this old fellow from all the dinners he has yet to come." For in Japan they say that all the turtles live to be a thousand years old. So the kind-hearted Urashima tumbled him back into the water, and what a splash he made! But from the spray there seemed to rise a beautiful girl who stepped into the boat with Urashima. She said to him: "I am the daughter of the sea-god. I was that turtle you just threw back into the water. My father sent me to see if you were as kind as you seemed, and I see that you are. We who live under the water say that those who love the sea can never be unkind. Will you come with us to the dragon palace far below the green waves?"

Urashima was very glad to go, so each took an oar and away they sped.

Long before the sun had sunk behind the purple bars of evening, Urashima and the Dragon Princess had reached the twilight depths of the under sea. The fishes scudded about them through branches of coral and trailing ropes of seaweed. The roar of the waves above came to them only as a trembling murmur, to make the silence sweeter.

Here was the dragon palace of seashell and pearl, of coral and emerald. It gleamed with all the thousand lights and tints that lurk in the depths of the water. Fishes with silver fins were ready to come at their wish. The daintiest foods that the ocean holds for her children were served to them. Their waiters were seven dragons, each with a golden tail.

Urashima lived in a dream of happiness with the Dragon Princess for four short years. Then he remembered his home, and longed to see his father and his kindred once again. He wished to see the village streets and the wave-lapped stretch of sand where he used to play.

He did not need to tell the princess of his wish, for she knew it all, and said: "I see that you long for your home once more; I will not keep you, but I fear to have you go. Still I know you will wish to come back, so take this box and let nothing happen to it, for if it is opened you can never return."

She then placed him in his boat and the lapping waves bore him up and away until his prow crunched on the sand where he used to play.

Around that bend in the bay stood his father's cottage, close by the great pine tree. But as he came nearer he saw neither tree nor house. He looked around. The other houses, too, looked strange. Strange children were peering at him. Strange people walked the streets. He wondered at the change in four short years.

An old man came along the shore. To him Urashima spoke, "Can you tell me, sir, where the cottage of Urashima has gone?"

"Urashima?" said the old man. "Urashima! Why, don't you know that he was drowned four hundred years ago, while out fishing? His brothers, their children, and their children's children have all lived and died since then. Four hundred years ago it was, on a summer day like this, they say."

Gone! His father and mother, his brothers and playmates, and the cottage he loved so well. How he longed to see them; but he must hurry back to the dragon palace, for now that was his only home. But how should he go? He walked along the shore, but could not remember the way to take. Forgetting the promise he had made to the princess, he took out the little pearl box and opened it. From it a white cloud seemed to rise, and as it floated away he thought he saw the face of the Dragon Princess. He called to her, reached for her, but the cloud was already floating far out over the waves.

As it floated away he suddenly seemed to grow old. His hands shook and his hair turned white. He seemed to be melting away to join the past in which he had lived.

When the new moon hung her horn of light in the branches of the pine tree, there was only a small pearl box on the sandy rim of shore, and the great green waves were lifting white arms of foam as they had done four hundred years before.

THE TONGUE-CUT SPARROW

In a little old house ill a little old village in Japan lived a little old man and his little old wife. One morning when the old woman slid open the screens which form the sides of all Japanese houses, she saw, on the doorstep, a poor little sparrow. She took him up gently and fed him. Then she held him in the bright morning sunshine until the cold dew was dried from his wings. Afterward she let him go, so that he might fly home to his nest, but he stayed to thank her with his songs.

Each morning, when the pink on the mountain tops told that the sun was near, the sparrow perched on the roof of the house and sang out his joy.

The old man and woman thanked the sparrow for this, for they liked to be up early and at work. But near them there lived a cross old woman who did not like to be awakened so early. At last she became so angry that she caught the sparrow and cut his tongue. Then the poor little sparrow flew away to his home, but he could never sing again.

When the kind woman knew what had happened to her pet she was very sad. She said to her husband: "Let us go and find our poor little sparrow." So they started together, and asked of each bird by the wayside: "Do you know where the Tongue-Cut Sparrow lives? Do you know where the Tongue-Cut Sparrow went?"

In this way they followed until they came to a bridge. They did not know which way to turn, and at first could see no one to ask.

At last they saw a Bat hanging head downward, taking his daytime nap. "Oh, friend Bat, do you know where the Tongue-Cut Sparrow went?" they asked.

"Yes. Over the bridge and up the mountain," said the Bat. Then he blinked his sleepy eyes and was fast asleep again.

They went over the bridge and up the mountain, but again they found two roads and did not know which one to take. A little Field Mouse peeped through the leaves and grass, so they asked him: "Do you know where the Tongue-Cut Sparrow went?"

"Yes. Down the mountain and through the woods," said the Field Mouse.

Down the mountain and through the woods they went, and at last came to the home of their little friend.

When he saw them coming the poor little Sparrow was very happy indeed. He and his wife and children all came and bowed their heads down to the ground to show their respect. Then the Sparrow rose and led the old man and the old woman into his house, while his wife and children hastened to bring them boiled rice, fish, cress, and sake.

After they had feasted, the Sparrow wished to please them still more, so he danced for them what is called the "sparrow-dance."

When the sun began to sink, the old man and woman started for home. The Sparrow brought out two baskets. "I would like to give you one of these," he said. "Which will you take?" One basket was large and looked very full, while the other one seemed very small and light. The old people thought they would not take the large basket, for that might have all the Sparrow's treasure in it, so they said: "The way is long and we are very old, so please let us take the smaller one."

They took it and walked home over the mountain and across the bridge, happy and contented.

When they reached their own home they decided to open the basket and see what the Sparrow had given them. Within the basket they found many rolls of silk and piles of gold, enough to make them rich, so they were more grateful than ever to the Sparrow.

The cross old woman who had cut the Sparrow's tongue was peering in through the screen when they opened their basket. She saw the rolls of silk and the piles of gold, and planned how she might get some for herself.

The next morning she went to the kind woman and said: "I am so sorry that I cut the tongue of your Sparrow. Please tell me the way to his home so that I may go to him and tell him I am sorry."

The kind woman told her the way and she set out. She went across the bridge, over the mountain, and through the woods. At last she came to the home of the little Sparrow.

He was not so glad to see this old woman, yet he was very kind to her and did everything to make her feel welcome. They made a feast for her, and when she started home the Sparrow brought out two baskets as before. Of course the woman chose the large basket, for she thought that would have even more wealth than the other one.

It was very heavy, and caught on the trees as she was going through the wood. She could hardly pull it up the mountain with her, and she was all out of breath when she reached the top. She did not get to the bridge until it was dark. Then she was so afraid of dropping the basket into the river that she scarcely dared to step.

When at last she reached home she was so tired that she was half dead, but she pulled the screens close shut, so that no one could look in, and opened her treasure.

Treasure indeed! A whole swarm of horrible creatures burst from the basket the moment she opened it. They stung her and bit her, they pushed her and pulled her, they scratched her and laughed at her screams.

At last she crawled to the edge of the room and slid aside the screen to get away from the pests. The moment the door was opened they swooped down upon her, picked her up, and flew away with her. Since then nothing has ever been heard of the old woman.

SHIPPEITARO

Brave Soldier was the name of a very brave man in Japan. One time he was going on a long journey. He had to go through woods and over mountains. He crossed rivers and plains. Near the end of his journey he came to a great forest. The trees were so thick and tall that the sun could never enter there.

All day Brave Soldier hurried along the mossy path that led among the great tree trunks. He said himself, "I must reach the next village before dark or else I can find no place to sleep tonight." So he hastened on along the narrow path.

After a time he seemed to be going up a mountain side. As he hurried on it seemed to grow darker and darker. Brave Soldier knew that it was not late enough for night to be coming on. "There must be a storm coming." said Brave Soldier to himself, "for I hear the trees sighing and rustling. Now I must hurry, for I do not care to be out in a storm."

So Brave Soldier walked as fast as he could, and hoped that he would soon come to a village. The wind rushed through the tree tops, and the rain hammered on the leaves far above him.

It was so dark that Brave Soldier could hardly follow the path. "If I do not soon find some house or village, I shall lie down here under the trees for the night. They are my friends and will not allow any harm to come to me."

He had no more than said this when he came to a clearing in the trees. It was not quite so dark here, and Brave Soldier saw some kind of a house standing in the middle of the open space. He went to it and found that it was an old ruined temple. It looked as though only bats had been there for a hundred years.

No palace ever seemed more welcome to anyone than this old ruined temple did to the tired traveler. He found the corner where the roof leaked the least, curled up in his cloak, and was soon fast asleep.

In the middle of the night a terrible noise awakened him. Such shrieking and yowling! It sounded like an army of cats, each trying to see who could make the most noise. When at last they stopped for a moment, perhaps to catch breath, Brave Soldier heard a voice say, "Remember, don't tell this to Shippeitaro. All is lost if Shippeitaro knows about it."

"I wonder what they are up to," thought Brave Soldier. "I will just remember that name Shippeitaro, for he seems to be quite an important person around here. It is possible that I may meet him some day." Then he turned over and went to sleep.

In the morning when he awakened, the storm was past and the sun was shining. Now he had no trouble in finding his way, and soon came to a village.

On all sides he heard a sound of weeping and crying. All were dressed in white, sign that some one is dead or dying.

"What is the matter? Who is dead?" he asked of an old man who sat by the roadside. Instead of answering, the old man pointed to a little cottage at the end of the street.

Some little children were sitting in the doorway of a house. Brave Soldier said to them: "Can you tell me, little ones, why all the people in this village are weeping?"

The children, too, only pointed to the same house at the end of the street.

When the soldier came to this house he saw an old man and an old woman weeping as though their hearts were broken. A little girl was trying to comfort them.

"Do not weep so, dear grandmother," she said. "I am not afraid to go. I am sorry to leave you, but some one must go, and the other women in the village will take care of you when I am gone."

"What is the matter?" asked Brave Soldier, coming up just then. "Where are you going and why are all weeping so?"

"I am going up to the temple to-night," answered the girl. "Every year some one must go or else the monster will destroy the village. There is no one else to go this year, so I will go. They will put me in that basket you see by the door, and carry me up to an old temple in the woods and leave me there. I don't know what happens then, for those who have gone have never come back."

Where is the temple?" asked Brave Soldier.

"It is up that hill in the woods, said the girl, pointing to the very temple where he had spent the night.

Brave Soldier remembered what he had heard there the night before, and he also remembered the name he had heard.

"Is there anyone around here by the name of Shippeitaro?" he asked.

"Shippeitaro? Why, that's our dog, and he is the nicest dog you ever saw, too." Just then a long, lean black dog came up and began to lick the hand of his mistress.

"This is Shippeitaro," said the girl; "is he not a fine fellow? Everyone loves him."

"Yes, indeed, he is a brave-looking dog," answered the man. "I want to borrow just such a dog as that for one night. Would you let me have him for so long?"

"If you will bring him back, for he must stay here to take care of grandmother and grandfather," said the girl.

Then Brave Soldier told her what he had heard in that same temple the night before.

"I mean to put that brave dog into the basket instead of you, and see what will happen. I will go along to see that no harm shall come to him." The dog seemed to understand what was wanted, and acted as though he was glad to go.

They put him into the basket which had taken so many beautiful maidens to their death. Just before dark they carried him up through the listening woods to the temple. All but the soldier were afraid to stay, but he took out his good sword and lay calmly down.

At midnight he heard the same frightful noises. He looked out and saw a troop of cats led by a large fierce-looking tomcat. They gathered about the basket and tore open the cover. Out sprang the good Shippeitaro, with every hair bristling. He seized the tomcat, who was really the monster, and made short work of him.

When the other cats saw their leader killed they turned and fled like leaves before the wind.

Then the soldier took the brave dog back to his mistress, and told the people how he had done what no man could have done, and saved the village from the monster.

Do you wonder that all the people love Shippeitaro, and love to have his picture over their doors? They think that it will frighten away   all   evil.

A GUIDE TO PRONUNCIATION

The division of a word into syllables is after a vowel instead of after a consonant, as in English.

Accent is very slight, as in French. It consists more in the length of the syllable than in the stress laid upon it.

Consonants are all very much softer than their English equivalents. This is especially true with *j*, which is pronounced more as though one started to give the sound of *z* but ended with *yu*.

a	has the sound of	a in father
e	"	ee in meet
i	"	i in it
o	"	o in stone
u	"	u in full

Both *e* and *o* are very much shorter than the English, *ē* and *ō* having about the duration of English *e* and *o*.

JAPANESE FAIRY TALES

Second Series

Retold by

Teresa Peirce Williston

1911

A FOREWORD

A story from the Land of Far Away! What mystery, what charm it holds for childhood! With quickened breath, with parted lips and shining eyes, the little voyager sets foot on the wonderful shore of Story Land.

Pulsating with interest, he greets the hero of that land, follows his adventures, and shares his struggles; learns the universal language of sympathy by sharing in the hopes and fears, the toil and the laughter of that other one, his brother now through the magic bonds of the story.

I have endeavored in this book, both through the illustrations and the "atmosphere" of the stories themselves, to bring the wee brothers from overseas as vividly as possible before the little folk of America. I hope the children who read these tales will see the beauty and charm of this life through the glamour of romance and the haze of tradition with which generations of story-loving Japanese have enwrapped it.

In collecting these stories I am greatly indebted to Mr. Katayama of Tokyo, and in planning the art work am under obligations to Miss Bertha Philpott of the Art Institute of Chicago for many helpful suggestions. Mr. Sanchi Ogawa, who illustrated the first series of Japanese Fairy Tales, has furnished the illustrations for this volume with the exception of the frontispiece and the cover design, which are by Mr. Kyohei Inukai.

The Author.

一種 灰毛ノモノ

THE FIRST RABBITS

The children in the sky were all crying. "Boo-hoo," said one. "Boo-hoo," said another. "Boo-hoo," said the rest.

"Children, children, what is the matter?" asked the fairy mother of the sky.

"We've nothing to play," replied one. "There's nothing to do," said another. "We can't play for there's nothing to do," said the rest.

"Why don't you twinkle the stars?" asked the fairy mother of the sky.

"The star lights are all put out," sobbed one. "The sun is shining and the star lights are out," sobbed another. "We can't twinkle the stars when the sun is shining and the star lights are out," sobbed the rest.

"Why don't you beat the thunder drums?" asked the fairy mother of the sky.

"The thunder drums are all broken," sighed one. "We've beaten all the thunder out of them," sighed another. "We can't beat the thunder drums for the thunder is all beaten out of them," sighed the rest.

"Why don't you shake the snow out of the snow sieves?" asked the fairy mother of the sky.

"It won't shake through the sieve," said one. "We've made the snow into balls," said another. "We can't shake the snow through the sieve when it's all made into balls," said the rest.

"Why don't you roll the snowballs?" asked the fairy mother of the sky.

"Oh, we will!" cried one. "Yes, we will," cried another. "Of course we will," said the rest.

Away they ran to the snowball field.

"Let's throw them," said one. "Let's toss them," said another. "Let's catch them," said the rest.

Up and down, this way and that way, back and forth, how the white balls danced and flew!

"Oh, look! They're falling through the sky floor," cried one. "They're all falling through the twinkle holes of the stars," said another. "They're falling through the holes down on to the earth," said the rest.

Away the snowballs jumped and bobbed. The star children all began to cry again.

Just then the fairy mother of the sky came with a torch to light the star lamps. "Crying again?" she said. "What's the matter now?"

"Our snowballs all fell through the sky floor," said one. "They all fell through the twinkle holes of the stars," said another. "They've fallen though the holes down on to the earth," said the rest.

"You naughty, naughty snowballs," said the fairy mother of the sky. So she threw her torch after them, but it only scorched their tails and turned them black.

Down on the earth they are hopping still, these soft white balls with their little black tails, and you children call them the rabbits.

LORD BAG OF RICE

A soldier in Japan was once about to cross a bridge near a lake when he saw a huge snake coiled on the bridge so that no one could pass. Now, do you think that this soldier turned and ran away, as many others had that day? No, indeed! He knew that a bridge was not the place for a snake, so he walked up and stamped on its head.

As he stepped on him, the snake was gone. Only a dwarf stood before him, who at once began bowing his head to the ground with respect.

"Now, at last I have found some one who is not a coward!" cried the dwarf. "Here I have been waiting for days to find a man who was brave enough to help me, but none dared cross the bridge. Everyone turned and ran at the sight of me. But you are strong-hearted. Will you do me a great kindness and save many lives?"

The soldier answered:

"I am a soldier of the Emperor, and I am here to save life and right wrong. Tell me your trouble and I will see what can be done to help it."

"There is a terrible centipede," said the dwarf, "and he lives in the woods on the mountain. Every day he comes down to the shore to drink. He dips his thousand poisonous feet into the beautiful water, turning it all foul and dirty. It kills all the fishes in the lake, too. I am the king of the lake, and I am trying to find some way to save my fishes."

"I do not know that I can help you," said the soldier, "but I will gladly go with you and try. "

The dwarf took him to his home in the bottom of the lake. It was a beautiful house, all made of coral and pearl. His servants, the crabs and sunfishes, brought them rice, fruit, and tea, served on tiny green leaves. The tea looked like water and the rice looked like sea-foam, but they tasted all right, so what matter?

Just as they were in the middle of their feast they heard a mighty roaring and rumbling. It sounded as though a mountain were being torn up.

"There he is!" he cried. "That is the noise of his thousand feet as they crunch on the stones of the mountain side. We must hurry or he will get to the water and poison it again. "

They hurried to the edge of the lake and saw the centipede already very near. He looked like an army marching with colored lanterns, for each one of his thousand legs glowed with many beautiful shades of crimson and green and gold.

The soldier drew his great bow and let an arrow fly at the monster's head. He never missed his aim, and the arrow struck the ugly head of the centipede, but bounced away. A second arrow flew, but that, too, bounced away.

He had but one arrow left and the monster was almost at the water's edge.

Suddenly he remembered that when he was a boy his grandfather had told him that if you wet the head of an arrow in your mouth it will kill any monster.

It took just a second to wet the head of his last precious arrow and send it whizzing at the centipede. It struck him on the forehead and he fell over dead.

Suddenly the soldier found himself back in his own house, which was now changed into a castle. Before him were five gifts, on each of which he read, "With the loving thanks of the Dwarf."

The first of these gifts was a huge bronze bell, on the outside of which was told in pictures the story of the centipede. The second was a sword which would always give its owner the victory. The third was a suit of armor so strong that no swords or arrows could go through it.

The last two were the most wonderful of all. One was a roll of silk of any color he wished, and the more he used of the silk the more the roll grew. The other was a bag of rice which never grew less, although he used all he wished for his friends and himself.

This last gift seemed so wonderful to the people that they called him Lord Bag of Rice from that day.

PEACH DARLING

Here once lived an old man and an old woman who had no child of their own. They felt very sad about this, for they said: "Who will care for us when we are too old to care for ourselves?"

Since they had no children of their own to love, they loved all other children and tried to make them happy. Even the cats and dogs, the birds and squirrels, knew they had friends in the old man and woman.

No cherry trees ever bore such beautiful blossoms as the ones by their cottage door, and all the bees of the village came to hum with delight at the long and graceful catkins on their willow tree.

One day the old man said: "To-day I must go to the mountains to cut grass. Oh, if I only had a stout young boy who could take this long journey for me! But then I must not complain, for we have each other." So off he went, happy and contented, in spite of it all.

Then the old woman said to herself: "If my good husband must take such a long, hard journey to-day, I, too, will be at work. I will take all these clothes down to the river and wash them."

Soon she was on the river bank, washing merrily, while the birds sang above her. "How jolly our little friends are to-day!" thought the old woman. "They twitter and sing as though they were trying to tell me a secret.

Just then something came splashing and tumbling down the river and caught among her clean clothes. The old woman took a stick and pulled it out. It was a huge peach. "I will take this home for my husband's supper; he will be so tired, and this will taste very good," she said. Oh! How the birds sang then!

That evening when the old man came home from the mountains his wife said: "Just see, here is a peach for your supper, which came floating down the river to me. I fancy the birds must have sent it, for they laughed and sang so when it came."

The old man said: "Bring me a knife, that I may cut it in two, for you shall have half of it."

When they opened the peach, there within it lay a tiny baby boy, as round and fat and smiling as could be. Because of his first cradle they called him "Peach Darling," and loved him as a child sent from the gods.

As he grew tall and strong they found that he was indeed wonderful. No one equaled him in strength, and none in wisdom. Every child in the village loved him, and all the birds and animals were his friends.

He took good care that his old father and mother should not have to work hard as they once did. "For," he said, "what better thing can I do than take care of you?"

When he became a young man he heard of the terrible monster, Akandoji. Years before, this monster had stolen a great deal of gold and silver from the villagers. It was said that he was so terrible that no one dared go against him, to try to recover the riches.

Peach Darling said: "I will go and fight this monster. Who will go with me?" But no one dared go, so he decided to go alone.

His father and mother were proud of their brave son, but their hearts ached to think of his going alone. His mother said to his father: "If you will grind me some fine millet seed, I will make our son some dumplings, for they may give him more strength to fight Akandoji." So the old man ground the millet seed, and the old woman made the dumplings.

Peach Darling put them into his pouch and started off on his journey. As he was going along a dog came up and sniffed hungrily at the dumplings. Peach Darling thought, "This poor dog is hungry, and I can do with one less dumpling. I am strong and shall not mind hunger." So he gave a dumpling to the dog.

As soon as the dog had eaten it he spoke and said: "Since you gave me of your food, I will go with you, for I cannot leave you alone." So on they went together.

Very soon they saw a monkey lying by the road, gasping as if in pain. Peach Darling stopped to see what was the matter and heard him saying: "Oh, if I only had a bite of something, l should not die." So Peach Darling took another dumpling from his pouch and gave it to the monkey.

After eating it the monkey was so much better that he said: "Since you have saved my life I will go with you, for I may be able to help you sometime." So the three walked off together.

As they were going, a pheasant hovered near them. Fearing that something might be wrong with her or her young ones, Peach Darling stopped and asked her what troubled her. In bird language she said: "Oh sir, my young ones are starving. I do not know what to do!"

"Do?" said Peach Darling. "Take them this dumpling, and if ever again you are hungry, come to me. I will not let you starve."

By this time they were down to the seashore, so they climbed into a boat and started off for the island of Akandoji. Just as they were starting there was a flutter of wings and the pheasant alighted in the boat with them.

"Dear Peach Darling," she said, "if you are going to face dangers, I will go, too, for perhaps I may be able to help you."

After a long row they reached the monster's island, and climbed the steep hill to the gate of the castle. Here they found the monkey of great use, since he always has four hands and four feet as well as a long, strong rope fastened to his body.

When they reached the great gate of the castle, they all four began to make the greatest noise possible. The man shouted, the dog barked, the pheasant screamed, and the monkey chattered, while they all beat on the door with stones.

The people within thought that a great army was upon them, so they threw open their gates and fled.

Peach Darling searched until he found Akandoji himself, who was just about to throw a great stone at him. He dodged the stone and picked the monster up in his arms, while the monkey tied him fast with ropes. When he found himself beaten, Akandoji agreed to return all his stolen riches. So his men carried down great bags of gold and loaded the boat of Peach Darling.

Then up went the sail, and as the wind swept them over the sea, the island of Akandoji grew small and disappeared.

All the village was glad when they returned, but none were so glad as the old man and woman. The people were now very proud of Peach Darling, and called him a great man, but he said: "Give all the honor to my three companions, for they did it all."

Peach Darling lived many years, and was always kind and wise. Many people of the village came to him for help.

Once the people brought him a wonderful peach fashioned out of gold. They said: "We all love you for bringing back our riches to us, but we love you far, far more for your wisdom and kindness to us."

THE OLD MAN WITH A WART

There was once an old man who had a wart on the side of his face. It was such a huge wart that it looked like a peach growing there. It hurt every time he ate his rice or drank his tea, but he never complained.

One day he was up in the mountains, cutting wood, when a dreadful storm arose. The pine trees, that usually murmured a soft and whispering song, now shrieked and groaned as the wind tore through them.

He found a hollow tree and climbed in. Here he was dry and warm while the rain poured down as though the very sky were falling.

He had never been in such a storm before, and as he listened to the wind, and breathed the fresh damp odor of the rain, he was glad he was there. The great pines, hundreds of years old, were bent and twisted about like grass.

The old man had thought he was the only one in the woods, but he soon heard voices of people coming nearer and nearer. "They must enjoy the storm," he thought, for they were singing and shouting most happily.

They did not sound quite like men, but more like the rushing of the wind and the hurried swaying of the trees.

They kindled a fire which leaped up in little sharp tongues of flame, for all the world like lightning. Each flash lighted up the forest, and then he saw that his jolly companions were the Storm Spirits. They sat in a circle around the fire and began their song. If you could but hear it!

It sounded like the wind whipping the tree-tops back and forth, or the breezes bowing the long grasses in lines before it. It was like great waves, trampling and tumbling upon the shore, or the pounding of tiny raindrops, hammering upon the dry leaves.

It seemed as though all the trees were swaying and bending in time with the wind because they loved it.

The old man could not sit still. He sprang into the midst of the group and began to dance. The air was sweet. The grass gave a faint fresh odor. He seemed to be dancing like the trees and flowers.

Like a willow by the river he bent and swayed and bowed. The song grew softer and sweeter until the trees were still and the sun peeped through the clouds. At last the old man sat down to rest.

Then the Storm Spirits said: "Oh, good man, come to us again and dance for us. As a pledge that you will come we will take this peach that grows on the side of your face. Is it not the most precious thing you possess?" So they took his wart and let him go.

When he reached home his wife cried, "Oh, husband, what have you done with your wart?" Then he told her all about it, and they were very glad.

These old people had a neighbor who had a wart on the left side of his face. This wart was red and shiny like an apple. He heard how the Storm Spirits had taken the other man's wart, so he, too, went to the mountain and crept into the hollow tree. There he waited until the storm came.

How it raged! The rain lashed the leaves like whips, and the lightning tore yellow gashes in the black clouds. This old man shivered and shook with fear.

At last the Storm Spirits saw him and dragged him forth to dance for them, but he was so frightened that he could only shake and tremble.

Then they were angry and said: "Well, if you can't dance better than this we don't want you any more." So they put the other wart on the right side of his face and started him off.

Poor man! He was sorry he came, for now he had a wart on each side of his face and was wet to the skin as well.

THE EIGHTY-ONE BROTHERS

Near Tajima, on the north coast of Japan, lived a mighty prince who had eighty-one sons. Eighty of them were bold, proud men, and hated the youngest brother, the eighty-first.

This youngest brother was kind and good to everyone. His elder brothers said: "That is not the way for a prince to act. You treat people as though you were the commonest wood-cutter, and not a cousin of the Emperor himself."

But in spite of all they said the youngest prince was just as kind to the people as ever, so his brothers hated him the more.

Now there was a beautiful princess in Inaba whom everyone wished to see. The eighty, brothers said: "Let us go and see this wonderful princess." So they started off, two by two. What a procession they made!

They took their youngest brother, the eighty-first, along to carry their bundles and wait on them, but he had to walk behind.

Over the hills and through the valleys they went until they came to Cape Keta.

Here they found a poor little hare without a scrap of fur on his body. Every bit had been pulled off, and he lay there with nothing to protect him from the hot sun.

"Oh, good friends," cried the poor hare to the eighty brothers, "I am nearly dying. Can you tell me what to do to make my fur grow again?"

The proud, cruel brothers only laughed at the poor hare, and answered: "You wish your hair to grow? Well, you just down and bathe in the salt water of the ocean, and then go and lie on a high rock where the sun can shine on you, and the wind can blow on you." Then they went on, laughing.

The hare did as they told him do. Oh, how the salt water stung his poor skin! Oh, how the sun and wind burned and cracked it!

He lay there groaning and crying with pain. Suddenly he heard some one calling: "What is the matter? Do you want help?"

"Oh, I am dying!" answered the hare. Then he heard some one climbing up the rocks, and in a moment more the eighty-first brother stood by him.

The poor young prince had so many bundles that he could hardly walk. "What is the matter with you? Why are you groaning so?" he asked the hare.

"It is a long story," said the hare, "and when I am through perhaps you will think I deserve what I now suffer, but I will tell you all. "

"I was on the island of Oki, and I wished to get over to this country, but I had no boat. At last I thought of a plan. I went down to the seashore and waited until I saw a crocodile raise its head above the water.

"Then I called, 'Croco-croco-crocodile, come here, I wish to talk with you.' He came up close, and I said, 'How many crocodiles are there in the sea?'

"'There are more crocodiles in the sea than there are buttons on my back,' said the crocodile.

"'But there are not so many of you as there are of us,' I said. 'There are more hares on the land than there are hairs on my back.'

"'Let's count,' said the crocodile.

"'All right,' I answered. 'You crocodiles lie here in a row from this land to Cape Keta and I will run across on your heads and count you as I go. Then we will count the hares and see which are the most.'

"So the crocodiles all came and lay in a row, and the farthest one just touched Cape Keta.

"I sprang on their backs and ran as fast as I could to Cape Keta, counting as I ran.

"How foolish I was! Just as I reached the last crocodile I said, 'You silly things! Do you think I care how many there are of you? You have made me a good bridge; that is all I wished. Thank you for it. Good-by.'

"The last crocodile caught me when I said that, and pulled every hair off my body.

"'We should like to know how many hares there are,' he said, 'so we will just count these hairs and see.' At that the whole row of crocodiles opened their great mouths and laughed."

"Well, it served you right for being so tricky, but go on with your story," said the eighty-first prince.

"Yes, I know it served me right for what I had done, and I shall never do that again," said the poor hare. "But after all my fur was gone, I was lying here crying when eighty princes came along.

"They laughed at me for my baldness, and told me to bathe in the salt water of the ocean and then lie in the sun and wind. I did so, and see how I suffer!"

The eighty-first prince felt very sorry for the poor hare, so he carried him to a spring of clear water.

"Bathe in this," he said, "and that will wash off all the salt. I will bruise some leaves, and the juice from them will make your fur grow again."

When this was done the hare felt as well as ever, and his fur began growing again.

Then the prince picked up his bundles and started on to catch up with his brothers.

When at last the poor tired boy reached Inaba he found his brothers already there, and very cross indeed.

The beautiful princess did not care to see them and they scolded the eighty-first prince as though it had been his fault.

They were just about to return home when a messenger came from the princess.

"Ah!" cried the first prince, "she wishes to see me; she is sending for me, I know."

"Oh, no! " shouted the second prince. "It is I whom she wants. I know she is sending for me."

The third prince fairly screamed: "You silly things! Don't you know I am the one she wants? I am far handsomer than any one of you. Of course she wants me."

The messenger waited until they were still at last, and then said: "Her Majesty, the Princess of Inaba, wishes the burden-bearer for the eighty princes to come."

The eighty-first prince laid down his burdens and followed the messenger.

He led him to the palace and into a room where sat the most beautiful woman he had ever seen. Beside her stood a hare whose fur was just beginning to grow.

The princess said to him: "My friend, I sent for you to thank you for what you did for my pet hare. He has just come to tell me about it. How does it happen that one so kind as you is only a servant?"

Then the eighty-first prince told her: "I am not a servant, O most beautiful Princess! My eighty brothers were coming to see you and made me walk behind and carry the burdens, but I'm just as much a prince as they."

"How can I repay you for all you did for my poor hare? Ask anything you wish and I will give it to you."

"The one thing I wish most of all is to live here with you," said the prince.

So they were the prince and princess of that land, and the hare was their companion.

As for the eighty brothers, they found they might as well go home first as last, and this time they had to carry their own burdens.

THE BAMBOO-CUTTER'S DAUGHTER

THE BAMBOO PRINCESS

An old bamboo-cutter was going home through the shades of evening. Far away among the stalks of the feathery bamboo he saw a soft light. He went nearer to see what it was, and found it came from within one of the stalks.

He opened the bamboo stalk carefully, and found a tiny baby girl. She was only a few inches tall, but as beautiful as a fairy. Indeed he wondered if she were not really a fairy.

He carried her home and told his wife how he had found her. They were very glad for they had no child, so they loved her as their own. In a few years she had grown to be a young woman. She was as sweet and kind as she was beautiful. A soft light always seemed to follow her.

When the time came to name her they called her The Bamboo Princess, because she was found among the bamboo, and because she was more beautiful than any princess.

People heard of how beautiful she was, and many peeped through the hedge at the edge of the garden in hopes of seeing her. All who saw her thought she was so lovely that they came back for another glimpse.

Among those who came often to the hedge were five princes. Each one thought The Bamboo Princess the most beautiful woman he had ever seen, and each wished her for his wife.

So each of the five wrote to the father of the princess asking to marry her. It so happened that all five letters were brought to the old man at the same time.

The old man did not know which one to choose, nor what to do. He was afraid, too, that if he chose one of the princes, the other four would be angry. But the princess had a plan. "Have them all come here," she said, "then we can choose better."

On a certain day the five princes came to the house of the bamboo-cutter. They were very glad to have another chance to see her, and each one thought he would be the one she would marry. The princess did not wish to marry any of them. She wanted stay with her dear father and mother. She wished to take care of them as long as they lived. So she gave each one something to do which was impossible.

The first she asked to go to India and find the great stone bowl of Buddha. The second one was to bring her a branch from the jeweled trees that grew on the floating mountain of Horai.

The third prince asked what he might do to show his love. The princess said that he might bring her a robe made from the skins of the fire rats.

She asked the fourth to bring a jewel from the neck of the sea dragon, and the fifth prince offered to bring her the shell which the swallows keep hidden in their nests.

The princes hurried away, each anxious to be the first to return, and so marry the beautiful Bamboo Princess.

THE GREAT STONE BOWL

People say that far away in India there is a stone bowl that belonged to the great god Buddha. They also say that it gleams and sparkles as though set with the most beautiful gems.

It is hidden deep in the darkness of a great temple. Few have ever seen it, but those who have can never talk enough about its beauty.

The prince who promised to go to India in search of the bowl was a very lazy man. At first he really meant to go, but the more he thought about it the lazier he felt.

He asked the sailors how long it took to go to India and return. They said it took three years. At that he made up his mind he never would go. The idea of spending three years looking for a bowl, an old one, too!

So he went away to another city and stayed for three years. At the end of that time he went into a little temple. There he found an old stone bowl sitting it, front of the shrine.

He took this bowl and wrapped it in a cloth of richest silk. To this he tied a letter telling of his long hard journey to find the bowl for her. Then he sent it to the princess.

When the princess read the letter she was sorry that he had suffered so much to bring her the bowl. Then she opened the silk wrappings and saw the bowl of common stone. She now saw that he had tried to deceive her, and was very angry.

When he came she would not even see him, but sent, the bowl and letter back to him.

The prince felt very sad, but he knew that he deserved it, so he went home to his own house. He kept the bowl to remind him that you get nothing good in this world unless you work for it.

THE BRANCH OF THE JEWEL TREE

The prince who was going for the branch of the jewel tree was very cunning and very rich.

He did not believe that there was a floating mountain called Horai. He did not believe there were trees of gold with jewels for leaves.

However, he said that he was going in search of it. He said good-by to all his friends and went down to the seashore. There he dismissed all but four of his servants, for he said he wished to go quietly.

It was three years before anybody saw or heard of him again. Then he suddenly appeared before the princess, bearing a wonderful branch of gold with blossoms and leaves of all colored jewels.

She asked the prince to tell of his journey. He made a bow and began his story.

"I sailed away from here," he said, "not knowing where to go. I let the wind and the waves carry me where they wished.

"We passed many beautiful cities and strange countries. We saw the great sea dragons lying on the water, sleeping as the waves rocked them up and down. We saw the sea serpents playing in the bottom of the ocean. We saw strange birds, with bodies like animals.

"Sometimes we sailed on with a gentle wind, and sometimes we floated with no breeze to move us for days and weeks.

"At times fierce storms arose. The waves rose mountain high. Wild winds whipped away our sails. We were driven and hurled to unknown lands.

"Again we saw great rocks on which the waves lashed themselves in showers of white foam.

"For days and weeks we had no food to eat and no water to drink. The great green waves lapping around us made us long for water all the more, but we could not drink the salt sea water.

"At last, just when I thought we would surely die, I saw a great mountain lifting its dark head out of the morning sea. We hastened to it. It was the floating mountain of Horai.

"We sailed around it several times before I could find a place to land. At last I saw a small cove and anchored there. When I went on shore there stood a most beautiful girl with a basket of food. She set down the basket and immediately disappeared.

"I was nearly starving, but I did not touch the food until I had broken off a branch from one of the jeweled golden trees, to bring home to you. Then I returned to my ship.

"The men were thankful for the food, so we feasted all day. In the morning, when the sun rose, the mountain had gone.

"A brisk wind was blowing, and in a few days we were home again. I came straight from the ship to bring you this."

Tears stood in the eyes of the princess to think of how he had suffered to bring her that jewel branch.

Just then three men came asking for the prince. "Could you pay us know?" they asked. The prince started to drive them away, but the princess told them to stay.

"What is it you wish?" she asked them.

"For three years we have been working to make this beautiful golden branch. Now that it is finished we want our pay."

"Where have you been these three years?"

"In a little house down by the seashore."

"Has the prince been with you?"

"Yes."

The prince was angry and ashamed. He knew that the princess would never believe in him again, so he went far away into another country to live.

The princess gave the jewel branch to the workmen to pay them for their years of work, so they went away happy, and praising the princess for her kindness.

THE FIRE ROBE

The third prince was to bring the robe made of the fur of the fire rats. He was rich and very much loved. He had friends in all parts of the world. He had one very dear friend who lived in China.

To him the prince sent a messenger with a great bag full of gold, asking him to find the robe made of the skins of fire rats.

When the friend read the letter he was very sad. "How can I ever do this?" he said. "Who ever heard of such a thing! Still I would do anything for Prince Abe, so I will try."

He sent messengers all over China seeking for the wonderful robe, but they all came back sadly, saying that they could not find it.

He sent to every temple, inquiring of the priests if they knew anything of this robe, and where it could be found, but the reply was always the same. No one had ever heard where it was, although everyone had heard that there was such a mantle.

He sent for all the merchants who went from place to place buying and selling. None of them knew of it.

At last he said to himself, "This robe that Prince Abe asks for is not to be found. There cannot be such a thing. To-morrow I will return his bag of gold to him, and tell him that I have searched my best but cannot find what he wishes."

The next morning, just as he was about to send the messenger back to Japan he heard a great noise in the street and looked out.

A great troupe of beggars was passing by.

"I will ask them if they have heard of this fire robe," he thought. So all the beggars were brought in.

They were surprised at being taken into the house of this great lord, and shown into the very room where he was.

He told them what he wanted, and asked if in their wanderings they had ever heard of this fire robe, and knew where it might be found.

They all stared at him in wonder. Some nearly laughed in his face. The idea of it! That he, one of the greatest lords in the country, should ask them, common beggars, for a fire robe.

One after another told him that they had heard of it, but it was only a story, for there was really no such thing.

Finally all had gone but one old man. He limped slowly up to the lord and knelt before him.

"My lord," he said, "When I was a child I remember hearing my grandfather tell about this fire robe. It was kept in a temple upon the top of a certain mountain, hundreds of miles from here."

The lord was delighted at this, but wondered why his messengers had not found this temple. He sent for the one who had visited the temples in that part of the country.

This man declared that there was no temple on that mountain. "There was in my grandfather's time," said the beggar, "for he had been there and had seen the beautiful fire robe with his own eyes."

The lord sent messengers to search out this mountain and find the temple at its top. The old beggar went with them.

When they reached there they found no temple, only a heap of stones. They searched around a long time, and finally found a large iron box buried under the stones.

They opened this box and found within it, wrapped in many folds of rich silk, a strange, beautiful fur robe. They carried it home joyfully to the lord, who was very glad to receive it, you may be sure.

He sent it as quickly as possible to the Prince Abe, who was no less joyful to receive it than his friend had been.

He took it out of the iron box, unfolded the rich silk wrappings, and looked with delight on the beautiful silvery fur. "Ah, how beautiful the Bamboo Princess will look in this!" he thought.

Then he remembered that every time this wonderful robe was put into the fire, it came out more silvery bright than before.

"It cannot be too beautiful for the lovely Bamboo Princess, so I will put it in once more, that it may be more beautiful for her than it has ever been for anyone else."

So he ordered a fire brought and laid the dazzling silver robe over the burning coals.

Like a flash the red flames leaped up, and before he could snatch it from the fire there was nothing left but silvery smoke drifting off on the wind, and silvery ashes dimming the red of the coals.

Poor Prince Abe! He was heartbroken. He could not blame his faithful friend, for he had done his best. He was glad he had not taken it to the princess before he knew it was the right one, for then she might think he too wished to deceive her.

He could only write to her telling her all, and then go away forever.

The princess was very sad when she knew what had happened, for she saw that this man was true.

She sent him a note asking him to come to her, but he had already gone away, so she never saw nor heard of him again.

THE SHELL IN THE SWALLOWS' NEST

The prince who was to find the shell hid in the swallows' nest was a very proud and lordly man. When he returned from the visit to the princess he called his head servant to him.

"Do you know anything about the shell the swallows keep hidden in their nests?" he asked.

The man stared. "The shell in the swallows' nests? Which nests?"

"I don't know. I want you to find out for me. I want that shell."

"Perhaps the gardener would know more about it. May I ask him?" So he called the gardener.

"Do you know where the shell is which the swallows keep hidden in their nest?" he asked the gardener. "No, I have not had it. Did you want it? I'll ask the water carrier if he has seen it." So he called the water carrier.

The water carrier said he knew nothing about it, but called another man. This man called another, and so on, until all the servants had been called. No one had ever seen the shell.

At last they asked the children. One little boy thought that he had seen one once. He had been up in the roof of the kitchen looking for swallows' eggs, and thought he saw a shell in one of the nests. Perhaps that was the shell the prince wished.

The prince was delighted and ordered his men to go and search the swallow nests in the roof of the kitchen. They went and looked, but said they could not reach the nests, for they were in the very top of the roof.

"But you must find a way to reach them," roared the prince, "Search every nest and do not come back until you have."

The men spent three days trying to climb up, but failed. At last they found that with a rope and a basket a man could be drawn up so that he could look into the nests. They searched and searched, but found no shell.

At last the prince grew impatient and went down to the kitchen himself to see what they were doing.

"Have you found the shell yet?" he asked.

"No, there is no shell there," the men answered.

Then the prince was furious and insisted on being pulled up himself to see. The men tried to persuade him not to do it, but he sprang into the basket and commanded them to pull him up at once.

The men dared not refuse, so they pulled him up. When he reached the nests the swallows began to peck at him, for they did not care to have all their eggs broken and their nests torn to pieces.

They flew at him so furiously that they nearly pecked his eyes out.

"Help, help!" he screamed. The men began to lower the basket. Just then he remembered the shell and thrust his hand into a nest. There was something hard there. He seized it, but lost his balance and came tumbling down. Instead of coming down in the basket he came down thump on the hot stove.

His men lifted him off as soon as possible, but he was badly burned and bruised. In his hand he held a shell, it is true, but it was a bit of eggshell, and the egg was spattered all over his hand and face.

He decided that this was all he wished of the shell from the swallows' nest.

By the time his burns and bruises were healed he had forgotten all about the princess, and he never climbed up to peep into the swallows' nests again.

THE DRAGON JEWEL

Prince Lofty was the one who was to go to bring the dragon jewel. He was a great boaster and a great coward.

Of course he intended to get the dragon jewel, but you may be sure he did not propose to take the trouble himself.

He called together a great crowd of his servants and soldiers and told them what he wanted. He gave them plenty of money for their needs and told them to be gone and not to show themselves again until they brought him the dragon jewel.

The men took the money quickly enough and went away, but not to find the dragon jewel. What did they care about it?

They did not believe that there was such a thing, and if there was, they were very sure the old dragon was very welcome to keep it. They did not care to try taking it away from him.

Meanwhile Prince Lofty was having a palace built for the princess. He did not doubt for one moment that he would win her, so he would have a house ready to receive her.

There had never been so beautiful a palace in that part of the country before. All the wood was lacquered, carved, or inlaid with gold and precious stones. The walls were hung with silks painted by the finest artists.

Then he waited for his men to bring the jewel, but they did not come. He waited a whole year. Then he was angry and decided that he would go himself.

He called together a few of his servants who were left and told them to fit up a boat.

The servants were frightened when they knew what he was going to seek. They begged him not to do it, for fear that the dragon would destroy them.

"Cowards!" cried Prince Lofty. "Cowards, watch me. Learn how to be brave from me. Do you think I will be afraid of any dragon? "

So they started, and all went well for two or three days. "Don't you see that the dragon is afraid of me?" boasted the prince.

That evening a fierce storm came up. The boat rocked and dipped. The great waves broke in foam over the side of the boat and they were all wet through. The rain poured down in torrents. The lightning flashed and the thunder growled and roared.

Brave Prince Lofty was sure the boat would upset. If they did not drown he knew that the lightning would kill them.

He huddled in the bottom of the boat seasick and frightened. He begged the pilot and the other men to save him. "What did you ever bring me to this place for?" he cried. "Did you wish to kill me? Is this all you care for the life of your great prince? Get me out of this at once or I shall shoot every one of you with my great bow."

The men could hardly keep from laughing, for it was only on his account they had set sail at all. As for shooting them, they knew he could not lift an arrow, much less pull the bow.

The pilot answered: "My prince, it must be the dragon who sends this storm. He has heard you say that you will kill him and take the jewel from his neck. You had better promise him that you will not hurt him, and then perhaps he will let us live."

Prince Lofty was willing to promise anything to have the storm stop, so he vowed that he would never touch the dragon, not even the least hair on the tip of his tail.

After a while the storm died down, the lightning ceased, and the waves were still. Prince Lofty was too sick, however, to know what happened until at last they came to a land. They lifted him out of the boat and laid him under a tree.

When at last he felt firm ground under him he wept aloud, and vowed that now he had something solid to rest on he would never leave it.

He was on an island far from Japan, but he would not return on a boat, not for a hundred princesses. So he stayed there the rest of his life.

The beautiful palace which he built for the princess had no one to live in it but the bats and owls, and sometimes a stray mouse or two.

THE SMOKE OF FUJI YAMA

Years passed by and the princess took good care of her old father and mother. They were very old now.

Now they saw why she had asked the five princes to do impossible things. She really wanted to stay with her parents, and yet she knew that if she refused to marry the princes they might be angry with her and harm her father.

Each day she grew more beautiful and more kind and gentle.

When she was twenty years old, which is quite old for a Japanese maiden, her mother died. Then she seemed to grow very sad.

Whenever the full moon whitened the earth with its soft light she would go away by herself and weep.

One evening late in summer she was sitting on a balcony looking up at the moon, and sobbing as though her heart would break.

Her old father came to her and said, "My daughter, tell me your trouble. I know that you have tried to keep it from me lest I should grieve, too, but it will kill me to see you so sad if I cannot help you."

Then the princess said, "I weep, dear father, because I know that I must soon leave you. My home is really in the moon. I was sent here to take care of you, but now the time comes when I must go. I do not wish to leave you, but I must. When the next full moon comes they will send for me."

Her father was sad indeed to hear this, but answered: "Do you think that I will let anyone come and take you away? I shall go to the Emperor himself and ask his aid."

"It will be of no use. No one can keep me when the time comes," she answered sadly.

However, her father went to the Emperor and told him the whole story. The great Emperor was touched by the love of the maiden who had chosen to stay with her parents and care for them. He promised to send a whole army to guard the house when the time came.

The old bamboo-cutter went home very cheerful, but the princess was sadder than ever.

The old moon faded away. A few nights showed only the blue of the heavens and the gold of the stars. Then a tiny silver thread showed just after sunset. Each night it widened and brightened. Each day the princess grew sadder and sadder.

The Emperor remembered his promise, and sent a great army who camped about the house. Hundreds of men were placed on the roof of the house. Surely no one could enter through such a guard.

The first night of the full moon came. The princess waited on her balcony for the moon to rise.

Slowly over the tops of the trees on the mountain rose the great silver ball. Every sound was hushed.

The princess went to her father. He lay as if asleep. When she came near he opened his eyes. "I see now why you must go," he said. "It is because I am going, too. Thank you, my daughter, for all the happiness you have brought to us." Then he closed his eyes and she saw that he was dead.

The moon rose higher and higher. A line of light like a fairy bridge reached from heaven to earth.

Drifting down it, like smoke before the wind, came countless troops of soldiers in shining armor. There was no sound, no breath of wind, but on they came.

The soldiers of the Emperor stood as though turned to stone. The princess went forward to meet the leader of these heavenly visitors.

"I am ready," she said. There was no other sound. Silently he handed her a tiny cup. As silently she drank from it. It was the water of forgetfulness. All her life on earth faded from her. Once more she was a moon maiden and would live forever.

The leader gently laid a mantle of gleaming snow-white feathers over her shoulders. Her old garments slipped to the earth and disappeared.

Rising like the morning mists that lie along the lake the white company passed slowly to the top of Fuji Yama, the sacred mountain of Japan.

On, on, up through the still whiteness of the moonlight, the long line passed, until once more they reached the silver gates of the moon city, where all is happiness and peace.

Men say that even now a soft white wreath of smoke curls up from the sacred crown of Fuji Yama, like a floating bridge to that fair city far off in the sky.

The Rōnin's Collection of Old Books:

Bushido, The Soul of Japan	by Inazô Nitobe
Japanese Fairy Tales	by Teresa Peirce Williston
In Ghostly Japan & *Kwaidan*	by Lafcadio Hearn
Japan, an Attempt at Interpretation	by Lafcadio Hearn

July 2018

Made in the USA
Las Vegas, NV
18 September 2021